SOCCER 'CATS

Secret Weapon

Matt Christopher

Text by Stephanie Peters
Illustrated by Daniel Vasconcellos

P9-DJA-359

Little, Brown and Company
Boston   New York   London

To Tracy van Straaten

First Edition

Library of Congress Cataloging-in-Publication Data

Peters, Stephanie.
    Secret weapon / by Stephanie Peters ; illustrated by
Daniel Vasconcellos. — 1st ed.
        p.   cm. — (Soccer Cats ; #3)
    Summary: Small for her age, Lisa Gaddy, the soccer team fullback, has trouble with her throw-ins from the sidelines until the coach devises a plan to turn her into a team asset.
    ISBN 0-316-13458-9 (hc) / ISBN 0-316-13475-9 (pb)
    [1. Soccer — Fiction. 2. Size — Fiction.] I. Vasconcellos, Daniel, ill. II. Title. III. Series: Christopher, Matt. Soccer Cats ; #3.
PZ7.C458Se   2000
[Fic] — dc21   99-31363

HC: 10   9   8   7   6   5   4   3
PB: 10   9   8   7   6   5   4   3   2   1

WOR (hc)

COM-MO (pb)

Printed in the United States of America

Soccer 'Cats Team Roster

Lou Barnes	*Striker*
Jerry Dinh	*Striker*
Stookie Norris	*Striker*
Dewey London	*Halfback*
Bundy Neel	*Halfback*
Amanda Caler	*Halfback*
Brant Davis	*Fullback*
Lisa Gaddy	*Fullback*
Ted Gaddy	*Fullback*
Alan Minter	*Fullback*
Bucky Pinter	*Goalie*

Subs:

Jason Shearer

Dale Tuget

Roy Boswick

Edith "Eddie" Sweeny

Chapter 1

Lisa Gaddy glanced at the scoreboard. 4–0. That would be a great score — if it were in favor of the Soccer 'Cats. But it wasn't. The Panthers were ahead and there were only ten minutes left in the game.

Lisa was miserable. At least one of those goals was her fault. As a fullback, she usually took the throw-ins after an opponent sent the ball over the side touchline near her. But Lisa wasn't very tall, and her throw-ins often fell short of their mark. One time, the Panther center striker had easily snagged the ball and sent it rocketing past Bucky Pinter into the goal. Now, anytime Lisa got ready for a throw-in, the Panther striker yelled to his teammates to crowd around her as close as they could.

For the moment, she was safe. The ball was at the other end of the field. She tried to concentrate on what was happening.

"Come on, Jerry! Come on, Lou!" she yelled to the 'Cats strikers. "Send it into the net!"

But neither Jerry Dinh nor Lou Barnes did that. Instead, a Panther fullback kicked the ball long and high, sending it back to midfield.

Halfback Dewey London charged forward to meet it. So did a tall Panther striker. The two battled for the ball. The striker won. With a swift kick she sent it to a teammate, who dribbled quickly down the sideline.

Bundy Neel tried to steal the ball away, but the Panther dodged him and headed straight toward the goal.

"Okay, let's stop 'em!" shouted Brant Davis, another fullback. He rushed the ball handler. The Panther panicked and made a lousy kick across the field. Lisa and another Panther tried to stop the ball, but it bounced harmlessly over the sideline.

"Lisa, take the throw-in!" Ted called to his sister. Lisa started toward the ball.

"No, let Alan take it!" a voice interrupted. Lisa stopped short. It was Stookie Norris, the third 'Cats striker. "Go on, Alan!"

"But Lisa's closest—," Alan started to say.

"Just take it, Alan!" Stookie shouted. Alan gave Lisa an apologetic look, then hurried to the sideline to accept the ball from the referee. With a swift over-the-head throw, he hurled the ball as far as he could. Stookie caught it cleanly against his chest and dribbled furiously toward the Panthers' goal.

Lisa took a few steps down the field, then stopped. Alan stopped alongside her.

"Uh, sorry about that, Lisa," Alan said, pushing his glasses higher up on his nose.

Lisa forced a grin. "Don't worry about it." Without another word, she ran back into position as play shifted away from the Panthers' goal.

Darn that Stookie! she thought. *Just because my throw-ins don't go as far as Alan's, that's no reason for me not to take them!*

Or was it? How would she have felt if her throw-in had been captured by a Panther instead of a 'Cat? Though she was quick and wiry, she was a few inches shorter than most of her teammates, even her twin brother, Ted. Unless she could add two inches to her height overnight, her throw-ins would never go very far.

And suddenly that seemed to be a very big problem.

Chapter 2

The game ended a few minutes later. Weary and disappointed at the loss, the 'Cats were quiet as they gathered their gear. All Coach Bradley said was that they had a lot to work on at practice the next afternoon.

Ted and Lisa walked home together. Lisa was silent until Ted jabbed her in the ribs.

"Give you a dollar if you tell me what you're thinking about," Ted said.

Lisa snorted. "As if you didn't know."

She was right. Most of the time, her twin brother knew exactly what she was thinking.

"Okay," Ted said, "so a couple of your throw-ins weren't that good. Big deal. You weren't the only one who made mistakes today."

Lisa kicked a pebble. "I know. But what if the other teams learn I'm lousy at throw-ins?" She kicked the pebble again. "Maybe I should just stop taking them. Stookie sure thinks I should."

Ted shook his head. "Stookie's wrong. If you're nearest to the ball when the other team sends it over the touchline, it's up to you to take the throw-in. Otherwise, the referee might think we're trying to delay the game for some reason."

Lisa knew Ted was right. In soccer, unlike most other sports, the time clock was never stopped, not even when the ball went out of bounds. When the ball did go over the side boundary, it had to be put back into play as soon as possible, or else time was wasted. The person taking the throw-in had to move fast.

That wasn't all. There were rules about how the ball was thrown. The player had to face the field when throwing, and his or her feet couldn't cross the touchline. At least part of each foot had to be planted on the ground when the ball was being thrown—no jumping up or running back and forth. And the ball had to be thrown with both hands from behind and over the head. You couldn't chuck it one-handed like a baseball, or toss it up underhanded.

Sometimes, Lisa worried that she wasn't going to do the throw-in right. That's when her throw-ins were the weakest. But how could she help that?

Once again, Ted seemed to read her mind.

"Coach Bradley said we've got a lot to work on tomorrow. Maybe throw-ins will be on the list. We'll probably do them over and over until we know just where and how to position ourselves perfectly." He grinned at his sister. "So quit your worrying and get ready to race me home! On your mark, get set, GO!"

With a peal of laughter, Ted took off. Lisa pounded after him. All thoughts left her mind except one: winning!

Chapter 3

Dinner that night was lasagna with buttered bread and crunchy salad. Lisa and Ted devoured everything on their plates, then helped their parents clean the kitchen. Since it was summer, they were allowed to either play outside for an hour or watch television until bedtime.

Unless it was raining out, they always played outside. At the start of summer, their father had brought home a big surprise—a huge trampoline! When Mrs. Gaddy raised her eyebrows, Mr. Gaddy had just shrugged.

"I always wanted one when I was a kid," he confessed. "And Lisa is so good at gymnastics I bet she'll love it." He was right about that. Lisa had been taking tumbling and gymnastics since she was four.

Mr. Gaddy showed Ted and Lisa how to use the trampoline safely. Soon all three were taking turns bouncing up and down, doing the splits, and landing on their backsides. They looked like they were having so much fun that their mother tried it, too. When she came off laughing, the twins knew the tramp was there to stay.

Ted was taking a turn first tonight. He stepped into the middle and started to bounce.

"I'm going to try a three-sixty!" he called. Lisa watched her brother bounce high and spin like a top, trying to make it all the way around before he touched down. As usual, he lost his balance and collapsed in a heap.

Lisa laughed.

"Oh, sure, laugh all you want," Ted grumbled good-naturedly. "But I'd like to see you do it!"

"I will, when it's my turn," Lisa replied, eyes twinkling. Thanks to her gymnastics classes, she had better balance on the trampoline. Both she and Ted knew it.

"Yeah, well . . ." Ted bounced some more, flailing his arms and legs in such a crazy way that Lisa couldn't stop laughing.

"Okay, your turn," Ted said, carefully lowering himself over the side.

Lisa stepped to the center. On her third bounce, she did a perfect three-sixty. Before Ted could say a word, she was up doing another, this time in the opposite direction.

"Show-off!" Ted yelled. Lisa knew he didn't mean it. She just kept doing three-sixties, first one way, then the other so she wouldn't get dizzy. She did the splits, too, and a couple of pikes, with her legs ramrod straight out in front of her and her fingers reaching for her toes.

While she was taking her turn, their father joined them. He watched Lisa for a moment, then called, "Have you ever done a somersault?"

"Not yet!" she yelled back.

"Aw, no way you've got the guts to do one of those!" Ted jeered.

"Oh, yeah?" Lisa retorted. She bounced a few more times. Then, taking a deep breath, she launched herself into the air, tucked into a ball, and flipped over. She didn't land on her feet, but she didn't care. She had done a somersault on her first try, and that was more than Ted could do!

"What do you think of that?" she crowed as she slid down off the trampoline.

Ted huffed. "Huh, bet if I spent all my free time tumbling around on gym mats, I'd be able to do one, too."

Mr. Gaddy laid a hand on Ted's shoulder. "Son," he said gravely, "until you can do a three-sixty without landing on your backside, stick to doing the splits. Now step aside, kids, and let a pro show you how things are done! Yee-ha!"

The fun on the trampoline had taken Lisa's mind off her soccer worries for a while. But when she crawled into bed that night, they all came crashing back.

How can I improve? she thought over and over. But she couldn't come up with any ideas. She could only hope that Coach Bradley would know what to do.

Chapter 4

Practice started at three o'clock sharp the next day. First drill of the day, Coach Bradley had them work on throw-ins.

"I need five players to spread out on the field." Lou Barnes, Jerry Dinh, Dale Tuget, Edith "Eddie" Sweeny, and Dewey London volunteered. "The rest of you get behind the touchline. You'll be taking turns doing throw-ins. I'm going to call the name of one of the players on the field. I want you to try your hardest to get the ball to that player."

Brant Davis was up first. The coach handed him the ball and called out, "Eddie!"

Eddie was about ten feet away from Brant. Brant fired the ball from behind his head directly to her. She caught it against her chest and let it fall to the ground. At a motion from the coach, she booted the ball back to him.

"Not bad, Brant. Next!" Alan Minter stepped forward.

"Dale!"

Dale was a good twenty feet away. Alan took a few steps back, paused, then trotted forward, lunged, and threw two-handed from behind his head. The ball landed near Dale's feet.

"Okay, good aim, but look down," Coach Bradley said. Alan did — and blushed. One foot was completely inside the touchline.

"If this had been a game, the ball would have been handed to the other side," Coach Bradley reminded Alan and the others. "Be sure to watch that."

Now it was Lisa's turn. Nervous about what had just happened to Alan, she decided not to run toward the line but to take the throw standing still.

Coach Bradley seemed to guess what she meant to do.

"Lou!" he called. Lou was standing the farthest away!

Lisa tried her best, but the ball fell far short of its goal. Lou hurried forward to retrieve it.

"Oh, brother," Lisa heard Stookie Norris mutter.

Miserable, Lisa waited for the coach to point out her mistake.

Instead, all he said was "Good try." For some reason, that made Lisa feel even worse.

Isn't he going to help me get better? she wondered unhappily.

Lisa did her best during the rest of the drill. Sometimes she hit her mark, other times she goofed up. Each time she messed up, Stookie had something to say. He was careful not to

let the coach hear him, but Lisa was sure the other 'Cats could. No one said anything, though—not even Ted.

"Let's gather 'round," Coach Bradley called at the end of practice. "Good efforts by everyone today. Friday, we play a game against the Tadpoles. See you then!"

The 'Cats all cheered, then broke to head for home. Ted and Lisa started off together.

"Let's see if any of the 'Cats want to use the trampoline with us tomorrow," Ted suggested. Brant Davis was walking with the coach right in front of them.

"Hey, Brant, want to come by our house and check out our trampoline tomorrow?" Ted called.

"I'll show you which Gaddy twin can do a somersault," Lisa added.

Brant gave them the thumbs up, then hurried off to where his father was waiting. Coach Bradley turned around and stared thoughtfully at Lisa.

"You can do a somersault?" he asked. "You're not afraid?"

Lisa shook her head. "I do that sort of stuff in gymnastics a lot—you know, flips and things. Want to see me do one?"

The coach nodded. Lisa handed Ted her gym bag. She took a few quick steps, then launched herself forward and planted her hands on the ground. Seconds later, she had pushed herself up and over and was standing on her feet again.

Coach Bradley clapped. "Beautiful!" he cried.

Lisa shrugged. "That was a front handspring. Learning to do that was much scarier than trying a somersault on the trampoline."

"Really? That's very interesting," the coach replied. He stroked his chin.

Lisa shot Ted a look. *What's going on?* the look said. Ted raised his eyebrows, as puzzled by the coach's sudden interest in Lisa's gymnastics as Lisa was.

Chapter 5

That night, Lisa and Ted were cleaning up the kitchen after dinner when there came a knock at the door. It was Coach Bradley. He was carrying a thin book under his arm. When he, Lisa, Ted, and their parents were all sitting at the kitchen table, he showed them the book. The tattered cover had a picture of a soccer player on it.

"I haven't used this rule book in a while because most of what I need to know is up here." Coach Bradley tapped his forehead. "But when you talked about doing flips today, it reminded me of something I'd read."

He thumbed through the pages until he found the one he wanted. "Here, read this part." He handed the book to Lisa.

Lisa read out loud. "'As long as the person taking the throw-in follows all the rules, there's no reason why he or she can't do a flip throw rather than a standing throw. But coaches should be sure the throw-in is okay with the referees before letting players attempt such a move.' " Lisa looked up at the coach.

"What does this mean?" she asked in puzzlement.

Coach Bradley took the book from her. "What it means," he said with a smile, "is that if you can learn to do a flip while holding a soccer ball, your throw-in problems are solved—and the Soccer 'Cats could have a new secret weapon!"

Ted frowned. "I don't get it, Coach," he said.

The coach laughed. "Picture this: Lisa retrieves the ball after it goes over the touchline. She takes a running start, then at just the right distance from the line, she flips herself over, still holding the ball. Just as she lands — her feet and body in proper position, of course — she releases the ball from behind her head and catapults it over the defense! The speed of her spinning body adds momentum to the ball and *zoom!* it goes higher, farther, and faster than she, or just about anyone, could ever throw it from a standing position."

"But if that's true," Mr. Gaddy said, "why doesn't everybody do flip throw-ins?"

Coach Bradley nodded. "Good question. Ted, name two other 'Cats who know how to do flips like Lisa."

Ted shook his head. "No one can."

"There's your answer. Not everyone does it

because not everyone *can* do it." The coach laid a hand on Lisa's shoulder. "And Lisa won't do it either, unless she wants to. It's up to her."

Lisa swallowed. Doing a somersault on the trampoline or a regular front handspring on the ground was one thing. But doing a handspring while holding a soccer ball, with everybody watching her . . . ?

Then she imagined herself lobbing the ball over her amazed defenders' heads. They'd be powerless to stop her! It would be just like the coach said—her throw-in would be the Soccer 'Cats' secret weapon.

She grinned at the coach. "I'll give it a try," she said. "Just tell me what to do!"

Coach Bradley grinned back. "Wish I could be the one to tell you," he said. "But I couldn't do a flip throw-in if my life depended on it. I know someone who can help you, though."

"Who?" Ted wanted to know.

The coach replied, "Bundy Neel's baby-sitter, Mary. I'll call her right now to see if she can work with you tomorrow, if you like."

"You bet I would!" Lisa cried.

Chapter 6

When the coach left that night, it was all arranged. He and Lisa would go to Bundy's house the next day.

The next afternoon, Ted tagged along with the coach and Lisa.

"Okay," Mary said when everyone was together. "Coach Bradley told me that you can already do a front handspring. That's all the soccer flip throw-in is, really. But instead of landing with your hands on the ground, you land on the soccer ball."

"Or on your back if you do it wrong!" Bundy started to laugh, but stopped when Mary glared at him.

"Sorry," Bundy mumbled.

Mary turned back to Lisa. "Okay, watch how I do this and see what you think."

Lisa paid close attention. Mary scooped up a ball. Then, before Lisa could blink, Mary launched herself down and forward, placed the ball on the ground, flipped her legs up and over, and pinwheeled back into a standing position. The ball was in perfect position for a throw-in: behind her head and held with both hands.

"And your feet are already planted firmly on the ground, just as they should be," Mary said. "All you have to do is hurl the ball into the air over the heads of your opponents to a waiting teammate!"

Lisa, Ted, and Bundy all clapped. "That was awesome!" Lisa exclaimed, picking up the ball. "Can I try now?"

Mary asked the coach to kneel down. Mary knelt opposite him. Both put their arms out until their hands were almost touching.

"Okay, Lisa," Mary said, "the coach and I are going to support your back and help you flip up to your feet after you kick your legs over. Don't worry about falling—we won't let you, will we, Coach?"

"No chance," the coach replied.

The first try, Lisa panicked. It felt so strange to land on a ball instead of her hands. Instead of going over gracefully like Mary had, she flopped to one side. But both Coach Bradley and Mary caught her before she could fall. The second try, she did better. By the thirteenth try, Mary and the coach were hardly supporting her back at all.

Ted and Bundy got bored watching her do the same move over and over. They went inside to play a card game and have a snack. They missed Lisa's twentieth try, when Mary declared she was ready for the next step.

"Let's see you throw the ball at the end of the flip," she said.

Again, Lisa had trouble at first. She couldn't seem to time the throw right. When she released the ball too soon, it shot straight up in the air. Too late, and the ball thudded into the ground in front of her and bounced away. Finally, though, Lisa got the hang of it.

"Okay, now let's work on aiming for a teammate. Coach, would you head downfield?"

As Coach Bradley jogged to the other end of the backyard, Ted and Bundy came back outside.

"Hold on," Bundy said. "You're going to try to reach the coach?" He shook his head in disbelief. "You've never thrown the ball that far in your life! No way are you going to make it to him!"

Lisa called back, "We'll see about that, Bundy Neel!" With a deep breath, she launched herself into a front handspring. The ball met the ground and her legs flipped up and over perfectly. Her upper body followed, and as her feet landed, she released the ball.

Bundy stared, open-mouthed, as the ball landed twenty-five feet from where Lisa was standing—right where the coach had positioned himself. Coach Bradley gave a whoop as he stopped the ball with his chest. Mary applauded madly. And Bundy walked up to Lisa, stuck out his hand, and said, "Put it there, Secret Weapon!"

Chapter 7

Lisa practiced her flip throw-in the rest of the afternoon. The coach, Mary, Ted, and Bundy took turns playing offense and defense. Eight times out of ten, Lisa's throws reached their mark easily.

They called it quits at dinnertime. Bundy couldn't stop talking about it, though.

"Wait 'til the other 'Cats see this!" he crowed over and over. "I feel sorry for our opponents!"

"We'll see, we'll see" was all the coach said. But he was smiling. "Now let's all get some rest. We've got to face the Tadpoles tomorrow!"

"No problem," Bundy said. "With Lisa's secret move, they won't know what hit 'em!"

Lisa wasn't so sure, though. It was one thing to do a flip throw-in during practice. But would she be able to do it in a game?

Guess I'll find out soon enough, she thought that night as she climbed into bed.

The next day shone bright and clear. The 'Cats took to the field in their yellow uniforms. All through warm-ups, Bundy chattered about Lisa's new move. "But," he said, throwing a protective arm around Lisa's shoulder, "she doesn't reveal the secret weapon until game time." The other players were curious but willing to wait and see her do it. Only Stookie Norris seemed doubtful.

"So she can do a flip while holding a soccer ball," he said with a shrug. "Big deal. What if she screws it up? I still say Alan should take any throw-ins on their side of the field. At least we know he can hit the mark half the time. She can't."

Lisa flared up. "I'm going to make you eat those words, Stookie," she hissed. Stookie just shrugged and walked away.

Lisa's anger faded as quickly as it had come. She tried not to think about what Stookie had said, but his words bit into her brain anyway. By the time the game started, she wasn't sure she wanted to try the flip throw-in after all.

Coach Bradley seemed to pick up on her worries. "Lisa," he said just as she took to the field, "if you aren't comfortable doing the move, don't do it. We can win this game without it."

The two teams took their positions on the field and the game began.

The 'Cats had won the coin toss. Stookie tapped the ball out of the center circle to Lou, who began a mad rush down the field. He dodged one defender after another, then got trapped in a corner. He tried to boot the ball back to Stookie, but a Tadpole fullback stole it. With a hard kick, he sent the ball soaring high overhead. It landed midfield.

It didn't stay there long. Dewey London raced forward and beat a Tadpole striker by a footstep. With a kick just as hard as the Tadpole fullback's, he sent the ball back into Tadpole territory. Moments later, Jerry Dinh rocketed it into the net. Barely five minutes had passed and the 'Cats were already on the scoreboard!

That early goal seemed to take the wind out of the Tadpoles' sails. The 'Cats scored two more times in the first half. The Tadpoles hardly got the ball into 'Cats territory at all.

Coach Bradley was pleased with his team's performance. "A real improvement over the last game," he said. "Offense, you're doing a terrific job. Defense, you haven't had much of a workout, but stay on your toes. Those Tadpoles could come out fighting hard in the second half." Lisa nodded with the rest of the team. She hadn't had to take a throw-in — yet. Secretly, she wished she wouldn't have to the whole game.

She didn't get her wish. As the coach had warned them, the Tadpoles came out raring to go. In the first few minutes, they stormed the 'Cats goal again and again, running circles around the defense. They were like a whole different team.

The four 'Cats fullbacks and goalie Bucky Pinter fended off each attack as best they could. Then came the moment Lisa had been dreading. She and a Tadpole striker were battling for the ball. The striker kicked it too hard, and it bounced over the touchline right near Lisa's feet.

Bundy's voice came across the field clear as a bell. "Okay, Lisa, let her rip!"

As Lisa trotted into position, she took in what was happening on the field: Stookie was

shaking his head in disgust. The Tadpole players were crowding around as close as they could, ready to steal the ball. From his position midfield, Bundy was calling, "I'm right here, waiting for that ball!" Lisa didn't miss the fact that a Tadpole player was laughing at what Bundy was saying.

Lisa panicked. *I can't do it, I just can't,* she said to herself. So instead of stepping back from the touchline to do a flip throw-in, she planted her feet and lobbed the ball weakly into the air. It came down in a patch of Tadpoles.

Tadpoles and 'Cats swarmed on it like bees on honey. But the Tadpoles had better position. They took possession and, five passes later, scored.

Lisa felt miserable. Bundy shot her a wounded look, Ted a curious one. But Stookie's look was the worst of all. His plainly said, "I knew she couldn't do it."

Chapter 8

That goal was the only one the Tadpoles made. The game ended with the score 3–1. Every 'Cat was smiling and laughing as he or she came off the field. Everyone but Lisa.

The coach pulled her aside. "Don't worry," he said. "You'll do the flip when it feels right."

Bundy was less understanding. "Lisa, why didn't you do it?" he demanded. "I feel like an idiot, telling everyone how great you were going to be. Then you choked!"

Stookie overheard. "You *are* an idiot, if you

really thought she was going to pull off some great new move," he scoffed.

Lisa was so humiliated, she couldn't speak. But to her surprise, she didn't have to. Ted spoke for her.

"She didn't choke and she can do it!" he said angrily. "She just wasn't ready, that's all. She only learned how to do it yesterday, for Pete's sake! When she is ready, she'll be great at it." He took Lisa's arm. "Come on, sis," he said. "Let's go home."

Lisa followed him, amazed at how he'd stuck up for her. But when she tried to thank him, he brushed it off. "No one talks to my twin that way," he said gruffly. Then he smiled. "'Cept me, of course."

All through lunch, Lisa thought about how Ted had stuck up for her. He didn't do that very often.

He believes I can do the flip, she thought. *Well, I'm going to prove he's right. And that means practicing until I can do it in my sleep. I don't want Ted to know what I'm doing, though, just in case.*

"Think I'll go upstairs and read for a while," she said, dumping her lunch plate into the sink. She hurried upstairs, careful to leave her door open just a bit. When she heard Ted turn on the computer in their parents' study, she sneaked downstairs, grabbed a soccer ball, and headed for the door.

Then she paused. She couldn't practice in their backyard because then Ted would know what she was doing. The playground? Too many other kids might be there—including kids from another soccer team. Finally, she picked up the cordless phone and hid in the closet. She dialed a number and waited impatiently for it to be answered.

"Hello?" a boy's voice said.

"Bundy? It's Lisa," Lisa whispered.

"Boy, am I glad you called!" Bundy shouted. Lisa winced, sure that Bundy's

booming voice had carried as far as the study. "Lisa, I'm really sorry for the way I blew up at you after the game. What Ted said was right. You'll do the flip throw-in when you're ready."

"That's why I'm calling," Lisa said, her voice still hushed. "Can I come over and practice the throw-in at your house?"

"Absolutely!" Bundy cried.

"Okay, okay, see you in a bit." Lisa hung up hurriedly. She cracked open the closet door and listened closely. She could just make out the sounds of Ted's favorite computer game. With a sigh of relief, she carefully put the phone back in its cradle, slipped out the back door, and hurried to Bundy's house.

Chapter 9

Later that week, the Soccer 'Cats had to cancel the game against the Scorpions because of rain. Lisa was disappointed. She had spent as much time as she could secretly practicing the flip throw-in. Only Bundy and Mary knew what she was up to. Now she'd have to wait two more days to show the 'Cats their secret weapon.

Finally, it was the day of the next game. Their opponents were the Panthers.

Before the game, Lisa quietly told the coach that she was ready. She held her breath while the coach checked with the referee that it was okay for Lisa to do a flip throw-in. Only when the coach gave her the thumbs up did she let her breath out. Then she pulled Bundy aside.

"I'm going to do it," she whispered. "Be ready the first time I take a throw-in. And be quiet!" she added in a hiss as Bundy started to cheer.

"Okay, team," Coach Bradley called, clapping his hands. "Now we all remember that the Panthers beat us pretty badly last time around. Well, this time it's going to be a different story, right?"

"Right!" the team yelled in unison.

You better believe it, Lisa added silently. *Panthers, you are about to be declawed. And Stookie Norris, get ready to eat your words.*

The Panthers had won the coin toss. The ref blew his whistle and the match began. The Panther center striker booted the ball to one of his wings. The wing hot-footed it down the sideline. Dewey and Bundy charged him simultaneously.

"Take him!" Bundy yelled to Dewey. Dewey did, performing a clean tackle from the side. But his pass to Bundy was wobbly. The Panther center striker swooped in and stole it. Dribbling madly, the Panther headed straight into 'Cats territory.

The fullbacks were ready. Brant and Alan hung back near the goal, keeping an eye on the wing strikers, while Ted and Lisa attacked. Their attack succeeded. With a strong kick, Ted sent the ball soaring to Jerry.

Back and forth the struggle went. First the 'Cats had control, then the Panthers. Just when it looked as if the Panthers would score, one of the fullbacks would manage to get the ball away. Or Bucky Pinter would make a terrific save and put the ball back into the 'Cats control.

Throughout the action, Lisa watched for a

chance to unleash her secret weapon. Finally, it came.

Deep in 'Cats territory, the Panther center striker got in trouble. He booted the ball to the sideline, looking for his teammate to capture it. The teammate missed and Lisa charged after it. Both she and the other Panther were too late, though. The ball bounced over the touchline. It was the 'Cats' ball and Lisa's throw-in.

"Hey, the little fullback's going to take her first throw-in," the center Panther called. "Get in as close as you can, team!"

Heart pounding, Lisa took the ball in both hands. She stepped a few paces back and looked for Bundy. There he was about thirty feet away, dancing from foot to foot—and totally unguarded.

Trying not to grin, Lisa rushed forward. The ball met the ground. Her feet flew up and over, and landed in perfect position just next to the touchline. As they did, Lisa launched

the ball. It soared in an arc high over the Panthers' heads and landed precisely at Bundy's feet. With a yelp of triumph, Bundy took off like a shot toward the Panthers' goal.

Stunned, neither the Panthers nor the 'Cats moved for a split second. Then Stookie took up Bundy's cry and charged downfield to help his teammate. The rest of the 'Cats' offense did too, followed closely by the bewildered Panthers.

"What was that?" Lisa heard one Panther ask another.

"That," Ted replied, barging in between them, "was the Soccer 'Cats' secret weapon! And that," he added, pointing downfield where a cheer rang out, "is called a goal!"

Chapter 10

Sure enough, there was Bundy, beaming with happiness at having made the first goal of the game. Moments later, the halftime buzzer sounded and the two teams left the field.

"Way to go, 'Cats!" Ted and Lisa yelled together.

"Way to go, Lisa! That was incredible!" There was Stookie, shaking his head and grinning.

Lisa grinned back. "I warned you I was going to make you eat your words," she said.

"I'd eat them again in a second!" Stookie replied. "Did you see the looks on their faces? Did you?"

"I was too busy seeing the look on your face." Lisa snorted with laughter. "Wish I'd had a camera!"

"What I want to know," said Ted, joining them, "is why could you do it this game and not in the game against the Tadpoles?"

Lisa threw an arm over her brother's shoulders. "I needed more time to get ready. You know all those days I said I was going to the library, or to the gym to do gymnastics, or wouldn't let you go to the pool with me?"

Bundy cut in. "She was really at my house, practicing! I'm the only one who knew she was doing it! And am I glad she did—that was the first goal I ever made!"

"Ahem."

Lisa, Ted, Stookie, and Bundy looked around in surprise. Coach Bradley was tapping his clipboard with his pen. With a raised

eyebrow but a gleam of merriment in his eyes, he said, "If you four are done slapping each other on the back, perhaps you'd like to join the rest of the team for our usual halftime chat. We haven't won this game yet, you know."

"Maybe not," said Stookie as he took his seat. "But with Lisa in there taking throw-ins for us, we're sure to show those Panthers who the top 'Cats really are!"